SQUASH, THE CAT

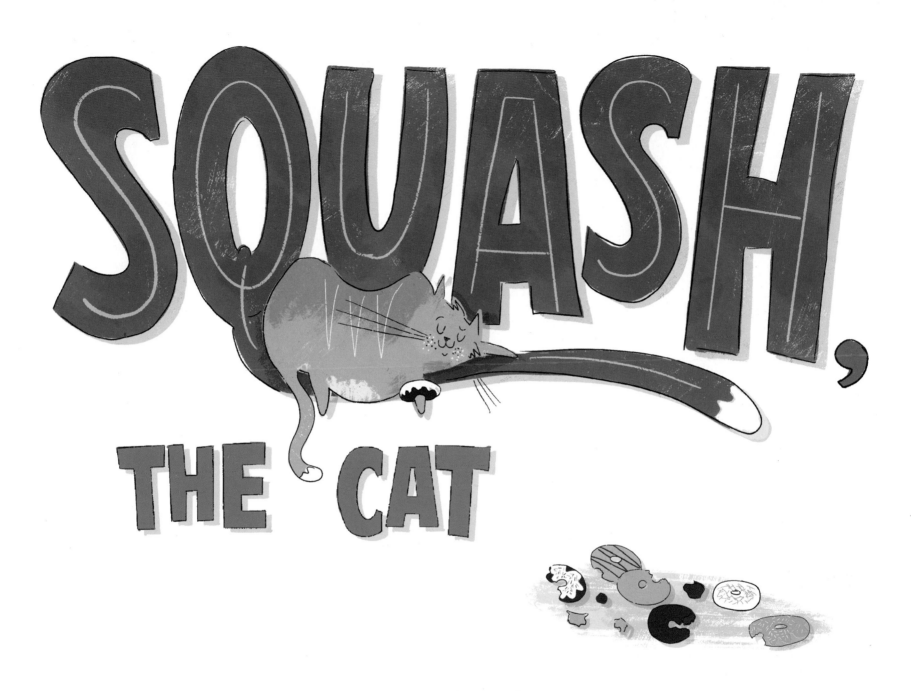

words + pictures by Sasha Mayer

RANDOM HOUSE STUDIO ▲ NEW YORK

This is Squash.

You might be able to guess how he got his name.

↗ SQUASH, THE FOOD   SQUASH, THE CAT ↗

Squash is an early-breakfast-followed-by-a-midmorning-nap

and-then-another-nap kind of cat.

Squash's best friend is Maggie.

Maggie is more of a wake-up-late,

followed-by-a-quick-skate

and-a-wild-playdate kind of girl.

Squash isn't always a fan of Maggie's adventures.

But that's okay, because Squash knows he and Maggie are still

perfect-for-each-other best friends.

Every morning, Squash teams up with Maggie so they can begin their day . . .

PERFECTLY.

Together, they are champions at curbing conflict,

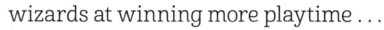

wizards at winning more playtime . . .

. . . and sensational associates

for all sorts of situations.

So naturally, the perfect-for-each-other best friend Squash
knows EXACTLY what to do when he sees Maggie being

devoured by a GIANT SNAKE!

But this time Squash makes a mistake.

An unbelievably BIG mistake.

Now Squash is a

can't-eat,

can't-sleep . . .

. . . can't-face-his-Maggie kind of cat.

And Maggie, well, Maggie is a wishes-she-had-her-tunnel-back kind of girl.

But . . .

. . . that's the thing about best friends:

they aren't always perfect.

And sometimes a little space . . .

. . . mixed with a little time

and an "It's okay, pal,"

is just what it takes to get back to being . . .

. . . perfect-for-each-other best friends.

To my boys: Mike, Jackson, and Cole

Copyright © 2023 by Sasha Mayer

All rights reserved. Published in the United States by Random House Studio,
an imprint of Random House Children's Books, a division of Penguin Random House LLC, New York.

Random House Studio with colophon is a trademark of Penguin Random House LLC.

Visit us on the Web! rhcbooks.com

Educators and librarians, for a variety of teaching tools, visit us at RHTeachersLibrarians.com

Library of Congress Cataloging-in-Publication Data is available upon request.
ISBN 978-0-593-56653-4 (trade) — ISBN 978-0-593-56654-1 (lib. bdg.) — ISBN 978-0-593-56655-8 (ebook)

The artist used Procreate and Photoshop to create the illustrations for this book.
The text of this book is set in 16-point Cabrito Norm Regular.
Book design by Nicole de las Heras

MANUFACTURED IN CHINA
10 9 8 7 6 5 4 3 2 1
First Edition